AF255269

Fateful Wish

Lupinski Clan Book Five

Emmy Gatrell

CONTENTS

Dedication…………………………………………………4

Chapter One……………………………………………5

Chapter Two………………………………………....14

Chapter Three…………………………………………25

Chapter Four………………………………………...31

Chapter Five………………………………………....39

Chapter Six…………………………………………46

Chapter Seven……………………………………...…57

Chapter Eight………………………………………65

Chapter Nine………………………………………...70

Chapter Ten………………………………………78

Chapter Eleven………………………………………...87

Author's Note………………………………………96

Thanks To…………………………………………97

Other Works…………………………………………98

Dedication

For my Grandma Edith

The original badass female Alpha

Miss you & love you bunches

Chapter One

My hands ached. I hadn't stopped ringing them or gripping whatever armrest I encountered since my escape from Scotland. It was the first time I was ever in a car, bus, or airplane, and everything about it felt unnatural. Gods and Goddesses' created shifters that could fly, swim across the ocean, and run faster than an automobile. Humans needed machines to do those things for them and I had to travel incognito so here I was, prepared to crash and burn. In more ways than one.

"Howdy folks, this is your Captain. We've begun our descent into Atlanta's Hartsfield International Airport. Please return to your seats and attendants begin your landing checks."

I loosened my grip on the armrest. "Thank the Goddess."

"First flight," asked the Mrs. Claus look-alike sitting next to me.

"Yes, first time for anything. I've never left home before."

Mrs. Claus patted my hand. "There's nothing to worry about, Dear. Think of something else, and you won't notice."

Great advice. Thinking leads to knots in my stomach about meeting the leaders of the Lupinski Clan soon. If they were anything like my Alpha back home, I could kiss my freedom and life goodbye.

The Lupinskis ruled us since the clan's inception over three hundred years ago. They naturally shift into what the Americans call Bigfoot, but they are so much more than that.

Forming an alliance and building a multi-shifter community would have been impossible without them. The Lupinskis alpha power can even force non-shifters to submit, and they have the ability to shift into most of the species they rule.

Stronger together than apart, the Clan flourished until a tragedy inspired the Good of the Clan law. One part of the law pertained to humans never learning of the existence of shifters. The sentence for breaking the law is horrific and my last memory of my father.

That night is seared into my consciousness. The sense of dread overwhelmed me before smoke permeated the air. How my heart pounded and stomach dropped when the front door was kicked open so hard it left a permanent dent on the wall. The terror when five of the more brutish 'security' officers burst into our home and restrained my father before he got out of his chair.

My mom and I jumped to our feet, and I ran around the table attempting to save him, but my mother stopped me halfway trying to keep me as far from the intruders as possible. Three of the brutes tied Dad with thick ropes; ankle to wrist, up and around his neck, back to his other wrist and ankle. If he struggled, the cord would tighten around his neck like Chinese finger cuffs and cut off his air supply.

I screamed for them to let him go as Reef put a hand around my throat and yanked me from my mother. His ever-present creepiness washed over my skin like an ice-cold shower leaving pinpricks in its wake.

Before my mother took a step toward us, Sven, who I called Uncle Sven since he and my dad were as close as brothers, grabbed mom and squeezed her into submission. At least, he had the decency to appear resigned yet uncomfortable. My mother and I stared at each other as our hands were bound and the cord wound around our necks. The end of my mother's linked to my dad and me to my mom, and then we were dragged out of our home.

Two men outside held torches for the others. They passed them out and flanked us with Reef in the front of the group ordering us to march to the center of the village.

The walk to the center of our village became scary and ominous for the first time. The light cast an eerie glow on the trees and the silence of night noises signaled that all creatures recognized nothing would be the same.

My father didn't make a sound, walking with purpose and pride. My mother's stride matched his, but as hard as I tried, my little legs couldn't keep up. In my haste, my foot caught a root, and I began to fall. Sven scooped me up and carried me the rest of the way.

When we reached the center of the village, every other adult was waiting in an incomplete circle which we went through and stopped near the raging bonfire. The crowd quieted when they saw my family, and once we were positioned, our escorts faded back enclosing us.

Our Alpha at the time, Angus, stared into the red, orange, and blue flames for several moments before turning to face us. The fire illuminated his face like Bela Lugosi. The scent of the dried moss being burned turned my stomach for the first time and ever since reminded me of death. Fear infiltrated our connected energy, except those who enjoyed the control they had over us.

"Sean has broken the Good of the Clan law!" Angus held up a newspaper with a blurry image of a plesiosaur. The headline read *London Surgeon's Picture of the Monster: Monster within yards of Lochside.*

My mother's cry resembled a banshee's call as she sunk to her knees. Every other member expressed either utter devastation or absolute hatred. The Good of the Clan law was the boogeyman to shifter kids. Used at bedtime or when we misbehaved, as the consequences for not acting appropriately.

My father's closest friend, Seamus spoke, "How can you tell that's Sean? The picture's so blurry that no—"

The Alpha's expression was unyielding. "Perhaps you want to take his place?"

Seamus appeared as if he would take the blame for a moment. Lucy, his wife, and my mom's closest friend was crying and holding tight to his arm. Out of the corner of my eye, I saw my father shake his head no, and Seamus reluctantly stepped back.

The photo on the front page of a human newspaper was the first proof that the Plesiosaurs did not go extinct with the rest of the dinosaurs. Although, humans never called us by our proper name, they gave us nicknames like, Champ, Ogopogo, Mokele-mbembe, to name a few. In Scotland we became the Loch Ness Monster, I hated it, we were not monsters. Although, calling us 'monster' worked *for* us in the early days, not so much now that humans are obsessed with the unknown.

The Alpha's voice boomed over the hush of the crowd, "The law has been broken, and I am obligated to sentence our 'Fate Worse than Death' punishment." Each sub-group of species had their own version of it, literally locked away only to be revealed when necessary. The mystery itself was enough to keep most shifters in line.

"Why are Edith and June here?" Someone from the other side of the bonfire shouted.

"Sean's family bearing witness of his execution *is* the Fate Worse than Death." Angus nodded, and Reef and Sven untied my mother from my father and led him to a shoulder height stake with chains bolted in the middle and the top.

My mother scooted closer and took my hands. "Edi, close your eyes and ears."

The situation clicked, and I finally understood what was about to happen. I tried to run to my father's side but snapped back because I was still attached to my mom. The wind was knocked out of me, but the binding around my throat prevented the air from escaping. The pain was excruciating, and the inevitable tunnel vision and bright flashes of light terrifying.

Mom tried to pry the ligature from my neck. She was crying and struggling to breathe since my reckless actions affected her too.

The sounds and sights around me were becoming blurred and distorted. I was close to death and then Lucy, a Djinn, appeared and placed her hands on us. "I wish for the binds of the innocents to be released."

The ropes around my mother and me fell; my father's did not. He was guilty.

Reef spoke out of turn and said mom and I should be retied, and Lucy tied up as well, but everyone else shouted to let us go. Angus ordered us to be left unbound. He didn't realize his concession marked the beginning of the end of his reign as Alpha and his life. While most of the pod admired his decision, it was a betrayal to the purists who had the physical strength to challenge his authority one day.

Angus told us to stand. Mom and Lucy obeyed. I didn't and kept my eyes closed. A firm grip lifted me until my feet dangled a couple feet off the ground. Reef relished the power he had over me. His smile gave me a chill as he set me on my feet staring straight ahead with one hand on my chin and another on my shoulder.

"My wife and child are innocent. Please, Alpha, don't make them suffer for my mistake."

"Every shifter will learn of your transgression. You put us all in grave danger, and I will uphold our most sacred rule. I will not kill your family, nor punish Lucy for her interference, but they will bear witness to your demise."

The men leading my father continued to the post. They wrapped the bindings around his neck and torso before walking away.

Angus surveyed the crowd, waiting until everyone was focused on him, and then his gaze locked with my father's and simply said, "Shift."

I screamed, "No, Daddy!" But my protest was useless against Alpha magic and power, so Dad shifted.

The chains tightened around his expanding form. I continued to scream, "Daddy, daddy, no, please don't leave me daddy."

He didn't acknowledge that he had heard me as he was trisected, around the middle and neck. His hands and feet were severed and dropped to the hard packed dirt but his head rolled and stopped near the Alpha's feet. My screams of daddy turned into wailing, but everyone else in attendance were too shell-shocked at the gruesome horror to do anything but stare.

It didn't take long for my dad's body to revert to human and he was looking right at me when it did. Reef pushed me out of his way and picked up the upper and lower halves of my father and carried them to the edge of the circle. The shifters moved out of his way, and he left where the light of the bonfire reached and then disappeared into the night. Alpha Angus ordered my father's head, hands, and feet staked around the village and then ordered everyone to go home.

Reef bragged the next morning about dumping my dad's body into a bog notorious for making things disappear. And a few days later, my dad's head, hands, and feet went missing from their stakes too. I always suspected my mom, but she never confirmed my suspicions, not even on her death bed.

Our pod was never the same; we became recluse and suspicious. Trusting no one, instilling stronger magic to keep us hidden. With the rise of technology, life became more dangerous. My poor mother had it the worst I think, she was a polar bear. Try explaining that if she showed up on camera in a Scottish Loch. I offered to move with her so she could live in a more hospitable environment, but it would be the exact opposite for my needs, and she refused to discuss it.

"Welcome to Atlanta," the loudspeaker crackled.

Mrs. Claus squeezed my hand. "Not so bad, huh?"

"Thanks, I guess thinking about something else worked,"

I lied, and she being clueless about the world I come from smiled, and then turned away to make a phone call.

Rehashing my father's death made me wonder if I would face a fate worse than death in the near future. Even though the Good of the Clan law was recently abolished, I did disobey my Alpha which was one of the biggest no-no's. I didn't know much about the current leadership, so I had absolutely no idea what their reaction to my story would be and what could happen next.

I turned my phone back on. Several messages dinged from my cousin George letting me know he was here and excited to meet me. I was happy that I would finally meet someone from my mom's family, terrified of what would come next. This was my

last ditch effort to get out of the mess I had gotten myself into.
These could be my final moments of freedom.

Chapter Two

The long walk through the airport and wait in customs produced a massive amount of butterflies in my stomach. Scenarios of what could happen grew exponentially worse each time the scene started over in my head. By the time I made it to where George said I'd find him, I was imagining the Lupinskis were waiting for me in the airport, ready to hogtie me and ship me back to Reef. Where facing a fate worse than death was less scary than what Reef would do to me first. What he was already planning. What I had run away from.

The giant poster board with, 'Welcome Edi' written across it in sharpie was unnecessary, it was incredible how much George resembled my mom. He was tall with a slightly rounded face and well built. Dark almost black eyes that sparkled like obsidian, a huge smile that made you smile in return, and he even had the same white streak in his hair she did, that I inherited as well. Somehow, that streak of white hair made me feel less alone in the world, it was proof I still had a family.

"George?"

"Edi?"

After I nodded he let go of the poster board and picked me up in a tight bear hug. "Awesome to meet you, Edi."

"Oof, it's nice to meet you too, George. I wish it were under better circumstances."

"You're here now, that's all that matters. Don't worry, my Alpha will get whatever is going on sorted out."

"We'll see. Hey, thanks for picking me up. But, you can put me down now."

"Sorry." He set me on my feet. "I'm excited, I never knew you existed."

"When I called two days ago you didn't sound surprised."

"My great-grandpa told me about you a week ago." George picked up, then crumpled the sign, and tossed it in a garbage can. He grabbed the handle of my suitcase. "Are you ready?"

I took a deep breath and nodded, "Ready as I'll ever be."

We walked out the door, and waiting at the crosswalk for a shuttle to pass I said, "George?"

"What's up?"

The street cleared and we crossed into the parking garage. "Why have you never heard of me? I never met you, but my mom told me all about her family. Because—" I mimicked how my mom said her favorite sayings. "—that's what bears do."

"Well, our families are related but very distantly. My great-great-great-grandfather was your great grandfather's nephew, and he was pretty young when your mom left. Plus, your mother's side of the family were constitutional purists." George put my luggage in the bed of a raised black beat up Ford and gave me a hand into the passenger seat.

"So what if they are?"

He shut the door, walked around, and climbed in. After starting the truck, he said, "They never spoke of your mother after she broke the Good of the Clan law and ran off with a dinosaur."

My jaw dropped and mind reeled as George left the parking garage. After, he turned on the biggest highway I ever saw, he glanced at me and asked, "Are you okay?"

"No. Please, explain."

"What?"

"How she broke the law?"

"You don't—" I shook my head, and he continued. "Shit, I don't know if I should be the one to tell you."

"Please, who else am I going to ask?"

"Okay. Um, from what my great-grandpa said, she was the last born cub to their species, the Polar Arctodus, and a potential Alpha. No one else had any cubs, she was their last chance of more. Her mate was chosen for the Good of the Clan to ensure your family's survival. The announcement and subsequent ceremony would have been during the conclusion of the bi-annual games."

"Where she met my dad."

George nodded. "They met that morning and ran off within an hour of meeting each other without telling anyone. No one realized they left until your mom didn't walk to the stage when called."

My stomach dropped and heart hurt, my mom and dad lied to me my entire life. They were two out of a small number of people that I thought never betrayed me, I was wrong. "What happened next?"

"The Alphas involved in choosing who she would mate with, forbade anyone to speak of the incident, your mom, or your father's pod ever again. The remaining members of her family blamed her for their demise, and they erased her. Not a single record or picture of her exists, and now they're gone."

"Demise? Did my mother's breed went extinct?"

"Yes."

"Because of what she and my father did!?!" *Oh my Goddess, my parents contributed to the extinction of an entire species!*

"No, it's not your parents fault. Your mother's breed had reproductive issues well before that. Your mother and father are not to blame, like any other couple who ran away to be together, or those forced together for that matter. Shifter mates are chosen by the Fates, we might be irrecoverably damaged from not following their will. Our former Beta, Abe Lupinski did the math, all shifters would be gone in the next two-hundred years if something didn't change."

"Sounds ominous."

"It is."

I fell silent letting everything sink in. Somewhat understanding why my mom and dad didn't give me all the dirty details. Knowing their decision contributed to the extinction of her species would be a massive burden to carry, but still... "Grrr... I can't believe I never knew they broke the law. With my situation, she should've told me."

"What situation?"

"It's a long and complicated story."

"Plenty of time before we arrive at Walt's bar."

"Your Alpha works?" I shifted in my seat to look at George and not how he weaved in and out of traffic in a nauseating fashion.

George nodded. "Of course."

"He doesn't live off the clan's fees and taxes?"

"What fees and taxes? We contribute to the general fund, but most of that goes to college scholarships, families facing unforeseen hardship, and donations to charities—"

"What about the taxes on your property, income, or produce?"

"We pay those to the US government—"

"They have a shifter tax!"

"That's ridiculous, of course not." He paused took a beat and then said, "What the fuck is a shifter tax?"

"Just another protection fee—"

"Your Alpha makes you pay a protection fee? That's his fucking job!"

"Reef considers it a service."

"A service!?! Protecting each other is written in our genetic code, especially for an Alpha."

I shrugged. "He's not a real Alpha, he won it by combat."

"But he is a real shifter!" The freeway changed, and the scenery became rural with occasional shopping centers off exit ramps. "I'm so sorry, Edi. It really sucks having to deal with shifters whose human selfish sides make the decisions."

"You sound like you're speaking from experience."

He nodded. "Unfortunately, I am. A couple months ago, my sister and her friends hurt a lion cub, and tried to kill Sydney, Nate Lupinski's fated human mate."

I covered my mouth in shock. Reef was evil, but not even he hurt children, except for me, of course. "What happened to your sister?"

"She didn't make it."

"I am—"

"Don't be sorry, she was always like that, there was something missing in her soul. She couldn't be saved, but they're trying to rehabilitate one of her co-conspirators."

"What does that mean?"

"No idea, that's way above my paygrade."

"There won't be any rehabbing of Reef. He's a sadist and sociopath who enjoys bullying me since I was little."

"Did he pick on you in school?"

"No, he's several hundred years older than me. He was creepy before but became a bully after what happened to my father—"

"What happened with your father?"

My mouth dropped. "You have got to be kidding me."

George turned right on a road that turned to dirt after a couple hundred yards. "About what?"

"Don't you know my father suffered a fate worse than death?"

"No shifter ever—"

"I witnessed his execution."

"For real?"

I nodded. "He was on the front page of the newspaper in nineteen thirty-four."

George glanced at me, "Holy crap! The Loch Ness monster picture? But I thought it was proven fake."

I shook my head. "That was my dad."

"And Reef has been a jerk since?"

"Yes."

"Is that why you're here? Did it escalate?"

I fiddled with my seat belt, not watching the road because we started going up a mountain with a road so narrow a strong wind could knock us off. "Yes and no. We need help, no one is strong or stupid enough to challenge Reef. He's an ineffectual and malicious ruler who destroyed my pod's spirit and brought us to the brink of ruin. The plan to seek help started a year ago, but was accelerated because of me."

"Why?"

"It was announced I would be his new mate for the good of the clan."

"The law was abolished."

"Reef made the announcement before."

George shook his head. "All declarations were voided."

"He doesn't care, he claimed I am his true fated."

"You can't claim that; either you are, or you aren't. That's the best part of being a shifter don't you think? Meeting our fated mate, and just knowing they are meant for you. I can't wait until I meet mine."

"Well, Reef used my situation to justify the declaration to the council and pod."

"Jimminy Christmas, what *other* situation?"

"My best friend, Jenn is a djinn. She granted me a wish not to let my memories affect my future."

He smiled and said, "That doesn't sound so bad considering everything you've been through."

"It wouldn't be but memories evoke emotions, so once a moment is over, I don't have those anymore."

George stopped smiling. "Wouldn't that make you a psychopath?"

I laughed, "No, but I can't ugly cry or belly laugh, that's enough to drive someone insane. Reef said because my feelings are dulled and corrupted, I wouldn't have realized that he was my mate. He lied about having mating symptoms and blamed his abhorrent behavior with women on me *not* fulfilling my obligation to become one with him, my fated."

"So sick, on so many levels. I can't believe everyone went along with it."

"Some of my pod were more than happy to blame me, and the ones who didn't, couldn't say anything. Shifters that vote or speak against Reef disappear, sometimes their entire family does."

"Why does he want you, I mean, not that he wouldn't, but with the bullying. I don't understand."

"I'm stronger than him."

"I still don't understand."

"I resist his commands with no effort. He thinks by mating with me, he'll gain strength."

"Reef would only receive a little boost of power that way."

"But, as his wife, I would be obligated to obey him including popping out as many children as possible. He'd get a power boost with each one, regardless of consent. He won't hesitate to use force; his right as a mate, and the way it works."

George gripped the steering wheel, "The way things work? Disgusting! Don't worry, Walt will be able to help you."

"You shouldn't make promises for your Alpha."

"I've got nothing but faith in him and the rest of the Lupinskis."

George turned left into an impassable stand of trees and I yelped and covered my eyes. After we completed the turn and didn't crash, I peeked through my fingers and saw that the trees disappeared and we were on a narrow road through a thick forest. "Was that fey magic? Do you have inmates?"

"Why would they be inmates?"

"For their magic."

"Fey are part of the clan, they do what is necessary to protect us."

"They're part of the clan? Reef falsely accused several of crimes and condemned them to lives of servitude to get what he wanted."

George turned into a packed parking lot of an unremarkable gray cement building with 'Walt's Bar' flashing in the window. "I hope Pixie is here, I don't think the local fey have any idea what's going on over there."

"I'm sure she is, this is a ton of cars."

"Nah, she'd teleport in."

"So, who do all of these belong to?"

"Everyone that could be here, is; news of your arrival spread."

"So... not a bunch of day drinkers."

"Some of them are, but no, they're here for you. You're a big deal." George got out and took my bag out of the back.

"Doubt I will be after they realize how much danger I put you in by running here." I opened my door and hopped down. Tried to smooth my wrinkled shirt to no avail and sighed at my frumpiness. I'll make a fabulous first impression while begging for my life.

Chapter Three

Before I could meet any of the hundred or so shifters, a couple of vampires, and several fey waiting to see me, George whisked me upstairs and ushered me in a spacious apartment, and then left shutting the door behind him. Although, it felt small with almost every member of the Lupinski family present.

The Clan's Alpha, Walt, met me at the door, a bit of a badass with his well-worn motorcycle jacket and black steel-toed boots. He beamed with love when he introduced his mate, Andy. She was stunningly beautiful and newly awakened as an Alpha, her tattoo, a continuous rose vine from ankles to neck. A tattoo like that, reflected how powerful she would be once she honed her power. In time, she would be strong enough to defeat any shifter without breaking a sweat.

Next was Nate, Walt's identical twin, but cleaner cut and his mate, Sydney. Her gold hair and eyes were a surprise; I didn't realize leprechauns migrated to the States.

Also present was the clan's former Alpha, Graham, and the previous Beta, Abe, with their fated mates, Melanie and Samantha.

And lastly, Ja'Lyn, the current Beta of the Lupinski Clan. She apologized for her husband, Henry, not being present; but looked relieved. If I were to guess, she's probably a victim of the Good of the Clan law, too.

When the introductions ended, there were a couple of knocks before the door opened and the most handsome man I ever saw walked in. Tall and built; shoulders rounded like boulders, tee-shirt stretched tight, sleeves about to split, and he stared at me as hard as I him. Someone said, "Jeff this is Edi."

The sound of my name snapped me back to reality. "Nice to meet you, Jeff."

"You too." He hesitated like he wanted to do or say something else but then sat in the chair furthest from me.

While I explained Reef's reign as Alpha, I avoided making eye contact with Jeff, too distracting. He growled when I got to the part about being declared Reef's fated mate, and by the time I finished, every other Lupinski growled too.

Mel broke the silence, "Did you know about any of this Graham?"

"No," Graham sounded regretful. "They were inactive members of the Clan when I became Alpha."

"But what about what happened to her father, Dad? How is it possible that someone within our ranks suffered a fate worse than death and we didn't know?" Ja'Lyn asked.

"My father was the Alpha in 1934 if he knew, he never told me."

Sam questioned Abe, "Why hasn't anybody gone to check on them?"

"The Lupinski Clan is not a dictatorship; we don't force shifters to join, but in hindsight, we should have gone to check on them. I'm so sorry." Abe seemed genuinely regretful.

"Don't feel bad. If you had made it in, you wouldn't be able to tell what was happening by observing. Reef would make sure everything appeared above board," I said.

"And he wants to mate with you," Jeff said between clenched teeth.

"Yes, he claimed I'm his fated…" I tried to glance at him quickly but got caught up in his eyes, my heart was racing, and I had lost the ability to speak, so I nodded my head.

I'm not sure how long we're staring at each other before Andy cleared her throat breaking the spell and I looked at her. She had a shit-eating grin on her face that quickly changed to guilt. "Edi, I'm so sorry you have all been living in this hell. But rest assured, we will take care of this. We won't let this injustice stand."

"I'm not sure—"

Andy cut Walt off, "Not sure? You are the fucking the Alpha, correct?"

"Yes," Walt sighed and grinned at the same time, it must have been an inside joke.

"Inactive members are still shifters, and we can't let these atrocities continue." Andy looked to the other Lupinskis, "We will fix this, period. Maybe we should take the rest of the day, and brainstorm."

"I thought I was the fucking Alpha," Walt teased.

"You are, and I'm the Alpha's Mate, and women get shit done." Andy replied and then shouted toward the door, "George, can you come in now?"

The door opened, George and several other shifters poked their heads in. "How can I help you, Alpha's Mate Andy, General of Getting Shit Done?"

Everyone laughed except me; I gasped because I expected Walt to rip George's head off.

Andy was still giggling when she said, "Will you put Edi's baggage in the back of Jeff's truck, please?"

"Sure thing—"

"Whoa, wait. Why is George moving my bag? I thought I'd be staying with him, you know, my family."

George answered, "Jeff has a decent sized pool, and you need water."

"You're exhausted. A shift might be what you need before we get to work on this tomorrow," Andy said.

"Tomorrow? I, uh—"

"As my mate so eloquently said, you should shift and rest. Jeff's the most powerful Omega on the planet, being psychically connected to every member can be overwhelming. Especially, with the recent changes in the clan. Perhaps some company whose every emotion isn't broadcast will give him some peace." Walt motioned to George, who nodded and disappeared back into the hallway.

"It's time for you two to go." Andy clapped her hands to get everyone's attention. "There's work to do. Nate and Sydney, can you reach out to our fey contacts and find out if there's a way to take down the pod barriers. Ja'Lyn contact the European Lupinski Clan chapter and grill them about what the fuck they knew, when, and *why* we were not informed. Abe and Mom, research what legal options there are. Graham and Grams, you're on battle plans. Edi, don't think about this again tonight, there's plenty of time—"

"Not too much time. Reef will discover I'm gone and retaliate against everybody I care about and helped me. I have to go back soon."

Jeff growled a little which shocked me but before I could say anything Walt stood from the couch and gave Andy his hand. "Okay, I think it's time for you two to go."

"But—"

"No buts, you rest, and we will figure out the rest," Walt said. "We're not letting you go anywhere near that poor excuse of an Alpha. We won't let any harm come to you."

"I'm more afraid for everyone else." Which was true, if the Lupinskis can't help me, I'd do whatever Reef wants as long as he didn't hurt anyone else.

George reappeared, "You're all set to go."

I began to stand from my cushy seat on the recliner when Jeff appeared in front me so fast it made me fall back down.

"Sorry." He chagrinned and offered his hand. A small jolt of electricity flowed through my body as he helped me up. He let go of my hand and motioned to the door with his head.

I glanced at everyone in the room and everyone in the hall. "Thank you all so much for helping me in any way that you can and welcoming me in such a loving and kind manner."

Smirks and a chorus of 'Byes' followed Jeff and me as we left the bar to his truck without saying a word. Talk about awkward.

Chapter Four

Jeff opened my door and helped me into the truck then asked, "All set?" I nodded because I was severely tongue-tied and couldn't speak. He shut my door then walked around, and climbed into the driver side.

Those two words were the only ones he spoke on the drive. He had given me side glances; I caught him staring and had to say, "Whoa," once when he started veering off the road but other than that, barely any interactions.

I have to admit I was staring at him myself. He was beyond gorgeous, and although my feelings were dulled, I had a slight tingle in the pit of my stomach. It was a bit confusing and had a passing thought of what it could mean but discounted it immediately because I had honestly believed I would never find my mate. I mean, who would want to be with someone who could never think of sweet memories and smile?

Jeff gripped the steering wheel with both hands, and I watched the muscles in his forearms contract and ripple like the waves in the lochs. I was so fascinated with the movement I hadn't noticed we had arrived until the truck rocked.

Jeff parked in front of a detached two-car garage to the left of his modest one-floor cabin in the woods. It was the house you drew as a kid. A door in the center, with two windows on both sides, and a triangle roof with a chimney. The porch started at one end and went around one of the corners to a wooden fence beyond. The home was adorable, but the landscaping exquisite.

The path was lined on either side with daylilies of every color and style imaginable. In front of the house a garden filled with roses. A fountain in the middle of the yard made with giant boulders, water ran over them into a small pond with water lilies. The feature was surrounded with orange, yellow, and red mums bursting like fireworks, and past that, a barren tree held a two-seater wooden swing moving in the breeze.

"Extraordinary."

"Thanks, it's my therapy. As Omega of the Lupinski Clan, I can be overwhelmed by everybody else's feelings, fears, and worries. That's why my house is so much further away from everybody else's. I still sense everyone's connected energy, but with less physical reactions. Different with you, though, I can sense you, but in subtle flashes."

"Once a moment becomes a memory, I can't feel it anymore so you wouldn't either. Curse of my wish."

"I like the flashes, especially when I touched you." He stroked his fingertips down the length of my arm to my fingertips and back up again. The feelings washed over me like a wave. Every nerve ending came alive as if he was touching me everywhere at once

I had tingles, excitement, and lust from looking at him and wanted to enjoy the fleeting moment, but an unwanted flash of nervousness came over me. Jeff moved his hand and within seconds, the sensations disappeared. "Do you want to see the pool?"

"I'd love to."

Jeff grinned, jumped out, and sprinted to my side. When he gave me his hand to help me climb down, those wicked feelings along my skin came back. After he let go, he grabbed my suitcase out of the bed of the truck, and led me inside.

The interior of his home was exquisite as the outside: heavy wooden furniture and a giant squishy black leather sofa and recliners, and fireplace with a carved mantle. A giant table surrounded by eight chairs and another two chairs were on either side of a matching buffet.

"I still need to make two more chairs to fit everyone in the family. I fell a little behind when my brothers, dad, and uncle all mated with their fated within one week."

I did the mental math. "You only have one more to make then."

"You're forgetting who's the most important to me."

"Who?" I asked but he didn't answer.

"Come on." Jeff turned and strode through a gorgeous kitchen and out the door next to the fridge.

The yard was enormous; beautiful bushes with red flowers covered the fence from this side. A lovely brick patio with a gas grill was to my right. To my left, a fire pit with chairs and lounges. In front of me was the biggest and most beautiful pool ever. It would hold at least fifty humans and another twenty in the Jacuzzi off the side, a stone waterfall as well as a slide, and a diving board.

"Beyond beautiful, but I'm afraid—"

"Of what?"

"That I might break something."

"Don't be ridiculous, the grizzlies and polars had an epic water polo match in there."

"I'm a lot bigger than a bear."

"Show me." Jeff's stepped in my line of vision with a smile that could melt girls' panties off. He took my backpack and purse, then walked several feet and put them on a chair. "According to Google you should fit, and I think taking a swim with you is a fantastic idea."

"What if a plane flies overhead? I'll be seen and how are you going to explain a dinosaur being in your pool?"

Jeff smiled then went to a metal box along the side of the wall and flipped open the front revealing a control panel and hit a couple buttons. He took my hand, and led me to the edge, bubbles from the jets caused ripples and steam. Glass panels began to rise on three of the four sides reached thirty feet above our heads, and sparkled as a shimmering magical barrier formed creating an arch.

"Wow, that's incredible."

Jeff laughed, "I landscaped several of the leadership fey properties. They were more than willing to help me not have a big ugly barrier ruining my aesthetic. They created the top for me.

From below I can make it show anything I want, and from above it looks like no one ever takes a swim. So, there's no excuse not to get into the water."

"But—"

"No buts. Get into the pool."

"I'm beginning to think you just want to see me strip naked."

Jeff didn't have the decency to say no as he grinned and shrugged his shoulders. The way his eyes were devouring me made me feel beautiful. I wondered if he would still make me feel the same way when he saw me naked.

I never stripped in front of a man before. Embarrassingly, I was still a virgin at eighty-six, but at the moment felt brave and decided there was a first time for everything.

"Okay, if you insist—"

"I insist."

"Don't say I didn't warn you." I walked about twenty-feet along the edge of the pool and took off my jacket tossing it to the side as I kicked off my flats. Waiting, until I turned around to unzip my jeans and stepped out of them as I took my shirt off.

Jeff took a step forward with an almost crazed expression on his face then grabbed his own thigh and squeezed for a second. Dark course hair spread along his hand and little pinpricks of blood where his claws extended into his own thigh muscle. I unsnapped my bra but left it on. With both thumbs, I hooked my panties and bent at the waist to pull them down and let my bra fall, and revealed myself to him.

Jeff body grew, hands and forearms furry, and blood trickled down his thigh. Happy with the effect I had on him, I dove in and swam underwater until I could stand on the bottom before I surfaced. Jeff had moved to the edge, arms crossed over his bare chest. I had no idea when he took his shirt off, but damn, I was grateful. My Goddess, he was spectacular.

"I'm still not sure this is a wise idea," I pleaded. He didn't understand, what would happen when I shifted in a pool versus a large body of water.

"Oh, I think this is a fanfuckingtstic idea."

"And what do you think is going to happen?"

"I'm not sure, but I can't wait to find out." He stared at my naked body underneath the water. "Show me."

Shifting came easy for me; just a thought for my body to shift. I did fit length and width wise, but Jeff forgot about volume. My expanding form pushed the water out into a giant wave dousing Jeff and the walls of the enclosure. The pool was deep enough to do a couple belly rolls, and let the magic restore my strength. When I surfaced, Jeff resembled a drowned rat and I laughed. I'm not sure how it sounded, but the glass shook.

I swam close enough to stretch my ten-foot long neck to him. Jeff stroked my cheek, "You are magnificent."

I enjoyed his touch and the look in his eyes for a moment before shifting back to human form. "And you're all wet. Can't say I didn't warn you." I laughed, and his expression changed. I pushed so much water out of the pool my jiggling breasts were exposed. Jeff growled and jumped in.

I was frozen in place watching his approach. He reached me and gazed into my eyes as he lifted his hand and stroked my cheek. Then skimmed his fingertips down my arm, threaded his fingers through mine, and touched his chest with them.

Soft and comforting, my body was at peace. Like as long as I was touching Jeff, I was normal, whole, and complete once again, but the sensations started to change. Throbbing in my clit reached a feverish pace as he teased my nipple into a tiny pebble. He nipped my earlobe, and my entire body shook with goosebumps.

"I uh—"

Jeff pinched my areola; stars burst behind my eyes and I gasped at the sensation. He moved both hands to my butt and pulled me closer then lifted me up high enough to wrap my legs around his middle. My clit landed over his erect cock relieving the throbbing for a few seconds before increasing in intensity. My body wanted more, my mind, however, was in a battle of wills. One side of me fighting for the impossible, the other rehashed old fears that I would never meet my—

"Mate," Jeff mumbled before he slammed his mouth down on mine.

I kissed him and wrapped my arms around his neck. Everywhere his body touched mine the sensations were almost overwhelming yet not enough. He pulled me in tighter against its length as he walked with me to the edge and ground himself into me.

I still wasn't convinced this was real. *What if this is a cosmic joke brought by the Fates to punish me for my original wish of not letting memories effect my future? The Fates don't like it when you mess with their design. Or what if—*

He stopped kissing me and gazed deep into my eyes, "I knew the moment I saw you, that *you* are my mate. Didn't you?"

I shook my head, "No, I thought you were hot. But I felt none of the normal mating symptoms until you touched me. I wouldn't be so doubtful if I could experience what you do."

"We wouldn't be mates if the Fates didn't have a plan for us regardless of your wish, trust that. Trust me." He squeezed my ass and pushed into me.

I wanted to, I wanted to trust him and the situation more than anything, but I didn't. I was stupid for making the wish. Frustrated I didn't experience our first meeting as he did; jealous he got to when I was dead to the world. "I wish I could feel how you feel—"

BOOM!

Chapter Five

The explosion came from where Jeff had set down my bag. Little pieces of clothing and other items rained down on my now destroyed suitcase. My best friend Jenn in her Djinn garb, standing victorious in the center of the mess with her arms out like she expected applause. "Knew you'd need me."

"What the fuck is going on?"

Jenn's wide-eyed expression at hearing a male voice lasted a second before surveying us and nodding her approval. "I thought Edi might need my help, so I stuck my lamp in her bag. Not sure why, the situation appears under control. Superior squat booty by the way. A bubble butt like that takes a ton of work."

Jeff ignored her, "Who is she and what is she doing here?"

"Hel-lo, I'm standing right here." The bell on her curl-toed boot jingled.

"Jenn, why are you wearing that?" She was in her Djinn uniform. It wasn't an outfit she had hanging in her closet, it was part of her magic, and only showed up when a wish required a shitton of power to grant. Sheer black harem pants, busty boobs spilling out of her low-cut midriff bikini top, accented with gold sequins and coins. A turban covered most of her bright red hair with a giant purple crystal hanging to the middle of her forehead, and shimmering golden tattoos stretched across her skin.

Jenn inspected the tattoos on her arm and poked one. It flashed brightly enough to make us all say, "Whoa."

"Holy crap, Edi! What did you do?"

"I wished I could feel what he feels." I pointed at Jeff's head.

Jenn eyeballed Jeff and took in our compromised state, then shrugged, smiled and said, "That might not be too bad."

"What the hell is going on? Edi, who is she and why is she standing in my backyard uninvited."

"Wrong, Buddy. I only show up like this when called to duty. It's part of my genetic code."

"What is that?" Jeff asked.

Jenn held her hands in front of her chest and batted her superior eyelashes. "I'm Jenn, Edi's best friend, plesio pod member, and a Djinn. I love long walks on the beach, magic carpet rides, and think people that hurt animals are meanies!"

"The genie whose wishes always go bad?"

"I am not a genie," Jenn said with the sneer. Genies were the offspring of a Djinn and Fey union, they got the perks but none of the inherent servitude of the Djinn. "My tortillas don't go bad, they just have minds of their own. Besides, I'm a little magical." She pointed at us, snapped her fingers, and our clothes appeared on our bodies but, we were in the pool, so they were soaked.

"Whoops."

"Not much though, huh?" Jeff carried me to the stairs.

"Not much what?"

"Non-wish related magic." He helped me out of the pool first, then himself, and shook off the excess water like a dog.

"Oh please, I'm not so bad! A stupid mistake because you got me riled up from the whole Djinn-Genie thingy."

Jeff put his hands on his hips and stared at Jenn until she said, "Whatever, I can fix it."

She snapped her fingers again and a hurricane force wind hit us. Any small decorative items flew from their proper places crashing against the back wall of the dome with some of the lighter furniture following. We had to grab ahold of the more substantial items as they slid past us, our legs lifted from the ground and we looked like a couple of windsocks. The wind stopped causing us to drop to the ground in a heap.

"All better!"

Jeff jumped to his feet and surveyed the damage, "All better!?!"

"Oh, I can—"

"No, I'll clean up myself later." He gave me a hand up.

"Are you sure because it's a snap—"

"Put those things away before you break something."

Jenn huffed, "Fine."

They stared at each other for a moment before Jeff asked, "Can you stop it?"

"Stop what, the taco?"

"Taco? What the hell are you talking about? Why do you keep talking about food?"

Jenn huffed, "Because I'm hungry."

Jeff clenched his jaw, he was getting frustrated with Jenn so I answered, "The W word isn't in the Djinn's vernacular. Too risky, so they substitute."

He looked at me for a second and then Jenn, "Okay, whatever, can you stop the taco?"

Jenn laughed, "No need for you to censor you don't have possession of my lamp. To answer your question, nope, rule one, once ground beef is made, it cannot be undone."

"I'm so sorry, Edi," Jeff said with a crack in his voice.

"Why are you sorry?" Jenn asked.

"Because of what Edi wished for." Jeff grabbed my hand. The horny mating feelings were replaced with fear.

"Feeling what you're feeling? How could that go wrong?"

"Jenn this is Jeff."

"Hi Jeff," she waved.

"He's an omega."

She grimaced, "Oh, so you have a psychic connection to the emotions of all the members of your what? Pack, nest, den—"

"Clan. I'm Jeff Lupinski, Omega of the entire Lupinski Clan."

"You have a psychic connection to every shifter on the planet… Oh, fucking hell. From one extreme to the other, huh Edi?" Jenn laughed, but concern clouded her eyes.

"Can we make another wish? I don't want Edi to go through what I do."

"I'm sorry, but there's nothing I can do, the future is already being rewritten." Jenn sighed, "You will begin to feel something within you Edi; no stopping it now. Do you remember the first time?"

"How could I forget?"

"This won't go easy for you, Edi. You'll feel the trickle of what's to come for now, and an hour tops before the Fates realign the future—"

"I'm sorry, what?" Jeff interrupted.

"The Fates, they can't revise the universe like this," she snapped her fingers. "Her lettuce is going to have far-reaching consequences, it'll take the girls—"

"What girls?"

"Duh, the Fates." Jenn rolled her eyes. "That whole bodybuilder not being the brightest bulbs stereotype isn't too far off, huh?"

"Jennifer!"

"Edith!" She waited for me to say something else, but when I didn't she said, "Listen Jeffy—"

"Jeff," he corrected.

"Whatever, cheese can have a minimal impact, or they can be like the butterfly effect where several... thousand... million lives need to be tweaked. It doesn't happen like in the movies where the world automagically resets. Like the world is an iPhone and the autocorrect feature is turned on. Can you imagine how many ducks would show up all over the world?"

"Ducks?"

"Who in the history of text ever said ducking right?" She laughed, Jeff didn't. "Never mind, what I'm trying to say is, writing the fate of mankind takes a personal touch, and the Fates take their jobs seriously." She examined her nails and mumbled, "Lazy bitches, so what if I give them so much more work." And making faces like she was replaying a conversation.

Jeff brought her back to reality. "You know the Fates?"

"Yeah, so? Been sent to the principal's office too. Listen, I only show up like this when the ramifications of the guacamole granted are at a cosmic level. Not a single lettuce master possesses the amount of magic required. It takes time to absorb what we need, and if we hold on too long, we blow up, literally, blow up." She mimicked an explosion with her hands and the appropriate boom noise.

"How much time do I have?" I asked.

"Not sure, when I start to resemble a disco ball it's go time. Instead of all this yapping, you two should enjoy this moment; you only meet your mate once."

"She's still not convinced she is."

"You don't need my mojo to convince her; you do know how this mating thing works, right?"

Jeff got a little smirk on his face, and a fleeting image of me laying back at the edge of the pool and his head between my legs filled my head.

"Oh, my." My body was on vibrate, and my breath became shorter. I didn't need any more convincing, and I kissed him. One of those earth-shattering, soul-shaking, eternal bond creating kisses poets wrote about since the dawn of time.

Jenn mumbled, "I guess he does know how the mating thing works. Don't mind me, I'm going to raid your fridge. I'm starving. One hour tops."

I didn't give a shit though, the over crazed mating feeling had subsided some to be replaced with peace and contentment. Jenn's words frightened me, his did too. After so many years of nothing, I would soon be overwhelmed with everything. I had no idea how I would feel an hour from now, but the only thing that mattered was the here and now.

Jeff lifted me off my feet, and I wrapped my legs around his back. He began striding with purpose but stopped when another explosion shook the ground. Jeff put me behind him to shield me from whatever was happening in front of us.

A voice rang out that sent chills down my spine. "I always knew you were a whore."

Chapter Six

"Reef," I said in disbelief to Jeff's back, and he tensed. I grabbed his shoulders and lifted myself to see over his shoulder. At the other end of the pool stood Reef surrounded by leftover purple magic mist. In his hand, an iron chain attached to a collar around Jenn's mom, Lucy's neck. She also wore her Djinn uniform, makeup streaked down her face, and she struggled to breathe.

"Let her go, now," I demanded.

"Who do you think you're talking to? How dare you speak to your fated that way!"

"I am not your mate."

"I declared it, and so it shall be. Do you need a civics lesson?" Reef paused, "Apparently you do, considering the lengthy list of your crimes." He began counting, yanking Lucy's chain with each number. "One, disobeyed your Alpha. Two, left the pod without permission. Three, not only did you leave, but you ran all the way to—" He scanned the yard with disgust "—this hellhole. Time to go!"

The tickle of pressure on my head made me roll my eyes. "Oh, stop embarrassing yourself. Why do you keep trying when your power doesn't work on me?"

"Does this?" Reef forcefully yanked the chain, and Lucy scraped her face on the cement when she landed.

"Let my mom go, she's innocent," Jenn pleaded.

"I know she had nothing to do with your stupid plan. My first wish was to identify your co-conspirators. She'd be dead too, if she helped you."

My stomach dropped. "Dead too?"

"What did you think would happen? That I would let Sven, Maria, Daniel, and Crystal go without suffering a Fate Worse than Death?"

"Oh my God—"

"I am your God as your Alpha and Mate, Edi. You were a fool to think you'd get away with betraying me. You will be punished for your actions and for me wasting two of my wishes on you."

"Two?" Jenn asked.

"Yes, two. One to identify who helped Edi leave, and the other to find her. Dragging you back to punish will be fun, but your pain won't replace my wishes."

"How did you get three wishes? There's no way my mom gave you her lamp."

"God, you're a stupid fucking bitch." Reef stared at Jenn and shook his head.

Jenn's confusion turned to anger when everything clicked. "You *stole* my mother's lamp!?! How dare you! Wishes are ours to give. We haven't lived in servitude for a millennia."

"I have a wish left."

"So?" Jenn threw up her hands.

"A well-worded wish will put you and the rest of your kind back in your place, as servants to men."

Jenn crossed her arms over her chest. "Be their sex slaves, you mean. Not possible."

"The amount of magic needed to enslave the Djinn is unattainable and unsustainable, even for Lucy, the most powerful Djinn alive," I said.

"True, she won't survive the granting, but it is possible. Leave with me now Edi, or I'll make my wish."

Help is on the way. Stall, Jeff telepathically said to me.

"If I go with you, how do I know you won't make your wish?"

Reef shrugged, "You'll have to trust me."

"I will never trust you. Forfeit your last wish by releasing Lucy, and I'll agree to go with you."

Jeff turned me to face him. *Stall, not surrender!*

I shook my head and tears filled my eyes, *I can't risk it.*

Try! Jeff pleaded.

My life for the freedom of the Djinn, there's no choice. If he takes the deal—

We don't know if what he's saying is true!

"What are you doing?" Reef yelled.

"Discussing the situation with my fated," I said without looking at Reef.

"Communicating telepathically doesn't mean that he's you're fated," Reef sounded frustrated.

"Then what does it mean?"

"Nothing, because I declared you will be my mate for the—"

"The Good of the Clan law is abolished," Jeff interrupted.

"I am the Alpha of the Highlands Plesiosaur Pod where my word is law. Who the hell are you?"

"Jeff Lupinski, Omega of the Lupinski Clan."

Reef grimaced, but a light bulb went off. "Then you should know the bylaws better than anyone."

"We are the law." I jumped at the sound of Walt's voice. Anger seeped from him. Andy on his right, had to fix Reef's wrongs. And on his left, a female water sprite was anxious to unleash hell when she saw Lucy leashed.

Whoa, how did I know what they are feeling? I thought.

Look at Jenn, Jeff answered.

The swirly shapes and intricate patterns of Jenn's golden tattoos began to pulse and shimmer. She was afraid the wish would turn out like everything else, horribly-horribly wrong.

What is happening

Your wish is being granted.

More shifters came into the backyard through the kitchen door, and I was bombarded with their feelings, so many of them it became painful.

Breathe through it, Edi. Try to focus your attention on one shifter at a time, Jeff instructed.

I did as he said and one-by-one focused on each shifter until I knew what they were feeling and then moved onto the next. For the first time ever, Nate regretted giving up being Alpha because he wanted to make Reef explode. Graham and Abe felt guilty for letting our inactivity go without question. Sydney, Melanie, and Samantha were upset by what they saw but unsure how they'd be able to help in any substantial way. The sight of Lucy in a collar and chain freaked Ja'Lyn out for an unrelated reason. A fey was ready to rip Reef's head off before going to Scotland and freeing his people from their imprisonment. And George needed to save me, his family.

"You have no authority over me," Reef yelled. "We aren't active members."

"You can't have it both ways. Using the bylaws to absolve yourself of criminal behavior while claiming you're not active, so I have no authority. But there's this." Walt focused on Reef, but I still felt the alpha power in the air when he ordered him to, "Let the leash go."

Reef dropped the chain like it was hot to the touch and his head tilted in submission. Anger turned to rage, and he said, "Fuck this. I warned you. I wish—"

The Water Sprite flicked her hand in Reef's direction. "Shush." His mouth kept moving, but no sound came out.

While Reef freaked out because he had a magical gag order, I said telepathically to Jeff, *I don't know what to do.*

Jeff took both my hands, *There is only one way to remove him as Alpha.*

An Alpha Challenge? I already told you, no one in our pod can best him.

But someone can resist his commands.

Are you insane? You think I should challenge him? He's twice my size and fights dirty.

Size doesn't matter when it comes to the challenge. Strength isn't your only tool.

What else do I have?

There's only one explanation for what you can do.

You think I'm an Alpha?

Yes, said Jeff. *Think about it Edi. What other reason could it be?*

He was right, there wasn't any other scientific or magical reason for my ability to resist Reef's power. *I'm an Alpha.*

Yes, now be what you're meant to be.

I nodded at Jeff and then turned to face Reef, who was still yelling on mute. "Reef, your abuse ends on the full Moon."

That's tonight, Jeff reminded me.

"Your reign of terror ends tonight—"

I meant to wait until next month!

Well crap, too late now. "Reef, I challenge you for Alpha."

Reef was stunned staring at me wide-eyed and slack-jawed.

"I'm going to let you speak again, but the moment you say the w of wish, the gag order gets placed again," the water sprite said. "Do you understand?"

Reef nodded, and she flicked her hand. The disorienting calm and dangerous ominous tenor to his voice unnerved me. "You dare challenge me? The daughter of the man who suffered a fate worse than death for exposing and providing proof of shifters to human?"

"My father made a mistake and accepted his punishment; it has nothing to do with me. I'm challenging you because you're an unqualified, ruthless bully who acts more like an abusive spouse than the Alpha the Scottish highlands Plesiosaur pod deserves and needs."

"The pod was a mess before I stepped into power."

"We weren't a mess, we were free! All you've done is isolate and use us for your own ego, gain, and laziness!"

"You think I'm lazy? I won this position by combat—"

"And that's the last time you broke a sweat."

Reef shrugged. "How do you want to do this?"

"A true Alpha challenge."

"You think you're an Alpha?" He laughed. "I won't break a sweat this time."

"Two go in, one comes out."

"No." Reef shook his head, "I don't want you dead."

"Well, I want to kill you."

"And I want your power for myself. If I win, the mating ceremony will be my victory celebration, and you will submit to me in every aspect for the rest of your life."

"And if I win, you'll be dead, so nothing else needs to be said."

Reef said through clenched teeth, "Do you accept?"

"I accept. Do you?"

"I do."

"It's settled." Walt stepped between us. "We will meet at the Harcourts' as the moon begins to rise. A shield will be erected to hide you from anyone flying overhead, and a couple of merfolk will stand by to observe what happens under the surface."

"No, they'll help her."

"I don't need to cheat, Reef. I agree with Walt, we need a witness."

"Then, I want to bring my own witness as well," Reef demanded.

"As long as they don't interfere, I don't have a problem with that."

Walt asked, "Are there any other terms?"

Reef responded, "Are you willing to perform the ceremony if Edi's bruised, bloody, and broken?"

"I'll hold up my end of the deal."

"Such fun I'll have breaking in my new mate." Reef glared at Jeff. "I think it may take me a long time and a lot of punishments to get her to learn her place, she's never been submissive." He did a half-assed head nod mocking his submission to Walt, "Alpha." Then grabbed Lucy's chain and they disappeared in a puff of purple smoke.

Jenn sunk to her knees crying, her tattoos were flashing brighter and longer. I ran to her and wrapped my arms around her. "It will be okay Jenn, I promise."

"How can you be sure? He's got my mom! If you lose you'll be his mate, your watermelon is going to be fulfilled any second, and it could kill you or me! I look like a statue in Trump Tower! I'm totally tacky in front of these people." She sniffed, "Who are all these people?"

"The Lupinskis, George, a fey, and a water sprite."

Jenn said to the sprite, "Thank you so much for that—" She wiggled her fingers around "—gaggy thingy you did."

"I'm Pixie, my pleasure." She gave us a smile and pointed to the male fey, "My mate, Baynard. We're going to get the lake ready. I think several different kinds of magic for the shield and surrounding areas is optimal Walt?"

"Whatever you think is best, kid."

Pixie rolled her eyes, "I'm three hundred years older than you. Should I call you infant?"

"I'd love to see you try." Walt made a ridiculous 'mean' face at her, she returned it, and almost everyone chuckled.

Jenn whispered to me, "She didn't call him Alpha."

"Yeah."

"They're teasing each other and goofing around? Reef would kill her and Angus wouldn't have been much kinder."

"This is a different world than what we've grown up in. I love it here."

"I think I do too."

Walt and Pixie had finished their playacting, and the male fey came over and joined them. "We should get going." They did a little hand wave to the crowd and were gone.

"Jenn," Walt helped her up. "I'm Walt Lupinski, Alpha of the Lupinski Clan."

"Alpha Lupinski, I'm Jenn jinxed Djinn of the Scottish Highlands Plesiosaur pod." She lowered her eyes and showed him her neck.

"Call me Walt, and don't do that, give me respect when I deserve it. Forgive my ignorance, but why do you resemble a seizure-inducing golden disco ball?"

"The wish," My voice cracked with fright, this didn't happen the first time. Jeff gave me a hand up and squeezed it tight. Walt's expression had me confessing, "It was an accident."

"Go on," Walt crossed his arms over his chest.

"Jeff and I were...um... discussing how he's my mate." Happiness spread through everyone. I tried to ignore everyone's feelings as they flooded me, but it was getting harder to do. "I wished to feel everything he does."

"Wow, went from one extreme to the other, didn't you?" Andy asked. "Aren't wishes supposed to be instant?"

Jenn replied, "Not when the future of mankind needs to be rewritten."

"What?" Everyone who had not been there for the explanation earlier said in unison.

"Somehow her wish affects everybody."

"Everybody in the clan?" Walt asked.

"Yes, and with how long it's taking, to grant, everybody on earth too..."

Questions faded into the background as the feelings of those present and further away increased in intensity. Anger, sadness, fear, contentment, regret, happiness, love, every conceivable emotion sliced through me.

My eyes locked with Jenn's and I focused on her. She was petrified, worried she killed her best friend. I tried to reach her telepathically, *Nothing's your fault. I love you.*

A single tear rolled down her face as her outline began to blur and became transparent and smoky. Only the top half of her body recognizable, a plume of smoke swirling below. The brightness of her tattoos was overshadowed when light shot out of her eyes, escaped the tips of her fingers, and streaked across the space between us. When she opened her mouth and screamed, light poured out and my world went black.

Chapter Seven

I snuggled in, so comfortable, safe, and loved in Jeff's arms. We were moving, in a van more than likely because of how many voices came into focus. I didn't need to hear them to know who because I could tell from their feeling. The nervousness within Walt, Nate, Ja'Lyn, Jenn, and Jeff, with a mishmash of love, anger, and fear, overwhelming and painful. Like getting thousands of papercuts each time a new one hit me.

The pain from feeling everyone's emotions will get better with time and practice, Jeff said telepathically to me.

So, it will get better? I won't automatically know what everyone's feeling are?

No, there's no way to turn it off. Just keep your eyes closed and practice focusing, so you are not overwhelmed with so many feelings at once.

"Was Edi's first wish like that?" Walt asked, still unsure of what he witnessed.

"No, although it did take a couple of minutes to absorb enough magic to complete. Thank the Goddess."

"What are we thankful for?" Nate hadn't been paying attention because he and Sydney were engaged in telepathic sexting.

"When mine are instant, they go whacky."

"How so?" Walt had a flash of nervousness expelled with cocky arrogance.

"Djinn wishes are exactly what you ask for, they must be worded precisely to achieve the desired result." Jenn said, "If I accidentally say the w-word, things get out of hand quickly. Hell, when I think them through they don't work out so well. When I was little, we lived in a Djinn joint—"

"A gin joint? Like a bar?"

"No, a community of Djinn," then under her breath, "Dumbass."

"What did you say to your clan's Alpha?"

"You have a nice ass."

A second before, I knew he would burst into laughter which made everybody laugh because he snorted. "Back to your story."

"Bossy."

"That's literally my job."

Jenn continued, "I was the only child in the Djinn joint, and out of loneliness I you-know-whatted that the family of mice living in my home could talk."

"Sounds awesome." Ja'Lyn lied because she felt mice were skinny rats, and rats freaked her the fuck out.

"Sure, at first, but mice have opinions on everything and they never, I mean never ever shut-up, ever. Their extended family is huge, and they all came. My house filled up with opinionated rodents who talked at all hours. We moved down the street, thinking the house would contain the problem, but I said home not a house, and the entire community was overrun."

"Ew," Ja'Lyn shivered.

"Needless to say, we weren't welcomed at the next joint, so we went to my dad's former pod in the Highlands, and met Edi. So, it worked out."

"What happened to the mice?"

"The Luchóg family still lives there, five hundred thousand generations at last count. The joint turned into a metropolitan mouse utopia, they're building a new high-rise complex."

"I'll make sure not to say the W word to you," Ja'Lyn laughed.

"Not how the system works. The only way for you to be granted one is if you have possession of my lamp."

The van slowed, there was a clicking noise, and we turned left. "Are the lamps hidden away like in Aladdin?" Walt asked.

"Before the revolution, anyone who found one, regardless of worth, received three wishes. The Djinn were treasure hunt prizes, or locked away and used as sex slaves or forced to make the most despicable human's dreams come true. My mother led the rebellion and won us our freedom. Now, we choose who we give them to."

"Why did you give your lamp to Edi?"

"Because her life got exponentially worse after her dad. She's more than capable of handling the bullshit Reef and everyone else put her through, if she healed. No one recognized PTSD back then, we thought my lamp was the only way for her to heal, but it worked too well and made her numb."

"After her wish to feel what Jeff feels, that won't be a problem anymore," Walt said. "Right, Edi?"

I sat up, a little embarrassed for being caught eavesdropping. "How long have you known I was awake?"

"The metropolitan mouse utopia. How's being an omega treating you?"

"Being an Omega? What are you talking about?"

"Your wish," Jeff said.

"To feel what you—"

"—Not what, you said how. You wished to feel how I feel, and being an Omega is how."

Jenn turned in her seat. "No wonder, the thingy took so long to grant, you're an Omega and connected to every single shifter on the planet."

"What about everyone else?" Ja'Lyn asked

"What about them?"

"You said granting the wish affected everyone on the planet, it changed the fate of the world. What happened?"

Jenn shrugged, "I don't know. The future was completely rewritten, and the only people that know we are living in an alternate reality were present when it happened. Unless, of course, you tell someone, but you shouldn't. Most folks don't react well, and some can become so obsessed with the idea and they lose everything or declared insane and locked up."

"How are you feeling, Edi?"

"I'm ready for this to be over."

Walt turned down a tree-lined driveway. "Good, because we're here."

"This is my father-in-law's property." Ja'Lyn hated him. "My brother-in-law, Gavin lives in there." She pointed to the right at a tiny log cabin hidden behind some trees. "His truck's not here."

Nate said, "He went to pick up Miles so he could finish the contract on the way. They should be here in twenty minutes."

"Contract? Aren't we doing things the old-fashioned way?" I asked.

"I don't trust Reef not to try and cheat even with witnesses. The contract only states what you both listed as your conditions. If he wins, you become his mate and submit to him. If you win, he's dead and the fate of the Scottish Highland Plesiosaur pod is within your hands. I also had Miles put a clause in about cheating and the forfeiture of lamps and wishes, and whatever else his brilliant legal mind can come up with. He's a human by the way."

"A human is coming to a dinosaur fight?"

"Two humans, a local witch is coming to bind the contract and hexes."

"Isn't it dangerous having them around?"

"No. Miles and I have been friends since college," Nate said. "He saw me shift once on accident and he never breathed a word. He's considered family. Witches are born with power, they may have human DNA but are still part of our magical community. We watch out for each other and help the other when asked."

We started passing cars lining both sides of the driveway, "Does your father-in-law own these?"

"No, these belong to Clan members. Gossip is lightning fast around here, plus it's a full moon and there's always a party."

"Did you tell them about the wish?" Jenn asked. She felt scared of us going through what we did with the last wish back at the pod.

Jeff answered, "No. The wishes are your business. It's up to you whether or not you tell others."

"We only spread the pertinent information," Ja'Lyn reassured us. "They are here to show you their support."

"Why would they care?" I was confused.

"Because they think you're a hero for what you're doing," Jeff told me.

"I'm no hero."

"Not true," Walt said. "You're putting your life at risk to save your pod, you are a hero." Walt parked next to George's truck. "Ready to go show the douche bag who the real Alpha is?"

"Fuck yes, I am." The other van pulled up as we got out and everyone began walking on the path leading around the ostentatious brick home.

When we turned the corner, I was shocked at the number of shifters in attendance and wasn't prepared. Being bombarded with a couple hundred shifters feelings caused me to sway.

Jeff put his arm around me to keep me steady. "Like before, try to focus on one and tune out the rest."

Taking a deep breath, I focused on a random shifter. After several seconds, I was able to filter the rest of the feelings from everybody else. It was easy to recognize the overall joy everyone got from being with one another. The underlying disgust with Reef. Guilt and shame that no one investigated when the pod all but disappeared, but, they had hope too.

Shifters of every sort were in attendance. Lions and tigers and bears, oh my, as well as falcons, wolves, primates, felines, canines, almost every shifter I'd ever heard of and some I didn't realize existed. They were laughing, joking, and enjoying each other. The joy from being together is what had been missing for most of my life even before what happened to my dad.

"You belong here." Jeff wrapped his arms around me from behind and pulled me back, so I was leaning on him. "As long as we are together anywhere will be home."

"What does that mean?"

"When you win, you'll be Alpha, and I will follow you back to Scotland."

"What if I don't want to be the pod's Alpha?"

"Why wouldn't you want to?"

I shrugged. "Not sure that's my path."

"Kick Reef's ass first, and then we'll figure out our future."

"He should be here by—"

A magical entrance announced Reef's arrival with a bang.

And then Jenn screamed, "What in the ever-loving fuck Reef?"

Chapter Eight

"Did you kidnap my father too, asshole?" Jenn skidded to a stop next to Jeff and me.

"Do not speak to me like that! I am your Alpha—"

"Not for long! What is my father doing here?"

"Don't worry, Baby Girl. I'm here on my own. When Lucy disappeared—" He glanced at Lucy, she still had a collar and leash around her neck, but she felt safe because of Seamus. "—we searched everywhere. When Reef showed up with your mother, we knew he stole her lamp. He still has control until his final wish or Edi defeats him tonight, and I'm not letting Lucy out of my sight again. I needed to make sure you two are safe, too."

"I'll be better when he's dead," I responded. "Are you okay, Lucy?"

"I'll be better when you kill him too," she replied.

"Are you finished?" Reef spat, "I'm ready to claim my prize, the moon is about to rise."

"I need you to sign this first." An attractive black guy handed Reef an official looking document and a pen. It must be Miles, the human Nate mentioned during the ride here.

"What the hell is this?" Reef shook the paper as he asked.

"A contract regarding tonight's events."

Reef hated reading and rolled his eyes. "Whatever." He snatched the pen, signed, and threw it at me. I added my signature and handed them back.

Walt joined us with a young lady wearing a long purple dress that matched her eyes, and a black cape with the hood pulled up over her head.

"What's the human kid doing here?" Reef glared at her.

"This is no ordinary kid," Walt said. "Lavender is the priestess of her coven, and the most powerful witch alive."

Reef huffed, "And why is she here? She's not part of the Lupinski Clan."

Walt held out his hand, and Miles handed him the document. "I thought someone without a horse in the race would be perfect."

"Perfect for what?"

Walt ignored Reef and laid the contract on top of his palm. The witch swiped her right hand over with a little finger wiggle. "Contract is bound! All set, Biggie." Walt raised his eyebrows, and she said, "You know, Bigfoot, Biggie? Get it?"

Reef interrupted whatever Walt was going to respond with, "What the fuck was that?"

"A little binding spell with consequences if the rules are broken," Lavender answered.

"What consequences?"

"A horrifying long and painful death of course." Lavender put her hands up like duh.

Reef emitted fear and anger because whatever he had planned was no longer an option. The bastard had intended to cheat.

"Are you two ready? I've got a curfew, and I'm not missing a dinosaur fight," Lavender said.

"I'm not sure your mom would be okay with you watching an Alpha challenge, it's to the death."

"Walt, she's my mom, but I'm her priestess. If she says anything, I'll turn her into a frog."

"Lavender," Walt said in a parental tone.

"Biggie?" Lavender gave him the look of the typical teenager arms crossed, foot tapping, annoyed expression, but when he didn't give in, she laughed. "I'm kidding, I wouldn't turn my mother into a frog or any other amphibian, a donkey maybe—"

"Lavender," Walt scolded.

"I told her I wanted to stay."

"And?"

"It's fine as long as I don't break curfew." She glanced at Reef and me. "You ready?"

"I need a minute," I told her with a smile. She is adorable even if she possessed the ability to turn me into a toad at will.

"Want to say your last goodbyes?" Reef teased.

I rolled my eyes, and Lavender slapped her hand over her mouth to contain a giggle. "I'll be right with you." She nodded, her eyes twinkling with mischief.

I went to Jenn first and gave her a big hug. "Kick his ass," she whispered in my ear.

"I will." Having known each other for most of my life and we knew what the other thought and didn't need to say anything else.

Jeff had calm confidence as I approached. He grabbed my hand, pulled me in tight and kissed me. The two of us connecting in a way only reserved for mates. The hoots and hollers from the crowd reminded me of why we were here. We slowed the kiss, and when we parted, Jeff put his forehead on mine and said telepathically to me, *I love you.*

I love you, too.

You've got this Edi. Be quick, I want to utilize the full Moon tonight too. Jeff sent me a vision of us making love, and biting me to make us one. It was so realistic there were little pinpricks on my neck where he'll make me his.

I laughed as I moved back from his arms. "I'll be back soon." I said and heard Reef acting like an ass mimicking me.

I walked with my head high and swaggered down the long dock with a large square platform at the end. It was a beautiful lake, almost a perfect circle with houses dotting the shoreline. The entirety of the surface was visible, but not the depth. It was probably quite deep. Merfolk tend to hang in the very bottom of the bodies of water so it made sense if they were landlocked they'd find someplace like this to live.

Dusk set in casting pink and purple shadows from the trees around the lake. House lights came on leaving shimmering light trails across the water. The night sound of bugs chirping accompanied the chatter from shifters giving a sense of excitement. Reef's footsteps grew louder, but I refused to give him the satisfaction of watching his approach and continued to scope out my surroundings.

"I have such big plans, you're going to be fun to break." Reef took off his shirt, trying to make a big show of his muscled body.

Ridiculous, like his human muscles, made a difference once shifted. I took off my clothes and peeked over my shoulder. Jenn was standing next to Jeff, they smiled and waved. I nodded and then dived into the cold water. I hadn't finished my first dive when Reef landed on my back, causing me to suck in two lungfuls of water. He grabbed my hair and straddled me like he was playing 'horsey'. The shock from getting jumped, his weight, and the water in my lungs had me disoriented, and free falling through the clear cold dark water.

Chapter Nine

The blindside would've worked with most plesios, but I'm no ordinary dinosaur. I'm a fucking Alpha. Shifting faster than ever before, forced off my back and he slammed into the sheer rock wall of the lake. The shock only lingered for a moment before beginning his own shift. He shifted quicker than the average shifter but compared to me, took an eternity.

I could have played dirty like Reef, but I didn't want any doubts about my victory. Instead, I used the opportunity to study the playing field, a magically converted marble quarry. It looked like the minors had dug down the center of a mountain in a giant circle for its minerals. The tool marks of the heavy machinery still withstanding the magical water and the bottom so vast I couldn't see it.

Reef finished shifting, began circling me, and I countered. He's largest of our kind at forty-nine feet from nose to the tip. His neck short, but muscular, and it wielded its head like a mallet, and four flippers blade-like, made it appear as if he could fly through the water. My nose to tail only spanned thirty-feet, but that made me more agile. I shot to the surface like a missile and did a flip as I sucked in a breath of air and reentered the water with Reef in my sight.

Plesiosaurs are apex predators, but we're also vulnerable and could be killed with a single well-placed bite. Our major artery runs the length of our neck protected by vertebrae and muscle, but you can tear through its protection at the correct angle.

We began to tease, using our deadly jaws and flexible necks to snap at each other from varying directions. Our tails could be used like daggers or bats depending on how they're wielded. If we use it broadside, whoever was on the receiving end would feel like they got hit by a truck, but the tip is sharp enough to puncture and slice flesh. Reef managed to tear the cartilage of my left back flipper. It hurt like a motherfucker, but I didn't let it faze me and earned one of my own along with his belly near his kidney.

Reef did a backflip through the water and circled underneath me. Coming in from below he tried to bite my injured flipper. I turned and used my tail to hit him square in the jaw sending him flying from the impact. He grew frightened, he deserved to be tortured a little before he got off easy with death.

Reef dove, and I pursued. Down we went, past where the light from above reached, and the temperature dropped. Thankful for the gulp of air I took, it should last me another ten minutes or so. Reef hadn't surfaced since we first entered the water. I didn't understand why he kept swimming away from the life-giving oxygen.

Being faster than Reef, it didn't take me long to overtake him. I knocked into him from behind biting his neck, but I missed the artery. He jerked in such a way my jaws released, and he went topsy-turvy tumbling to the lake floor.

He used his tail to push off and picked something up in the process. And he flung a ball looking thing at me, which broke apart and a thick substance hit me. Numbness set in where it touched and spread to almost complete paralysis of my entire body. Unable to move, I sunk to the bottom.

Reef swam above me laughing in my head. *I can't believe it worked again.*

Again? Is this how you defeated Alpha Angus? By cheating?

Reef ran his tail the length of my body. He moved his head closer to mine. *Do you want to see what I did next?*

You forgot something.

What?

You signed a contract with a cheating clause.

Who is going to see? None of the observers are in the water, we are alone.

What difference does that make? It was a magical contract.

Bound by a child. Besides, who will enforce it if nobody is here to witness what I'm about to do to you?

"Oh my God, Dude, so not true." If I weren't paralyzed, I would've jumped at the sudden specter of Lavender floating and glowing between Reef and I. "And screw you, too." She crossed her arms, huffed, and stomped her foot on nothing.

What the Fuck? I heard in my head from Reef, and Lavender did too because she responded.

"My power was prophesized, Numbnuts. I am the most powerful witch alive, and you are a fucking idiot to think you outsmarted me." Lavender glanced at me, "Please don't tell my mom I swore? I'm broke and can't afford to pay the swear jar again this month."

Not a problem, I replied telepathically.

"Thanks." She smiled at me and glared at Reef. "Just so you know, I projected the fight above us on the camouflage shield. And since I am the most powerful witch on the planet, I included audio of what you two have telepathically said too."

Reefs expression remained neutral, but his emotions broadcasted loud and clear. He knew he was fucked.

"They aren't the only ones. The Lupinskis thought your pod should bear witness, so it's being broadcast there as well. It was in the contract." Lavender gave an evil grin and let the implications sink in.

Soul shaking fear rushed through Reef. Not only had everybody witnessed his attempt to cheat, he also admitted to using an illegal means to kill our last Alpha. While Angus wasn't perfect, he didn't deserve to be killed in such an undignified manner.

"Walt's never going to let me hear the end of this," Lavender said.

The end of what? I asked.

"He and Graham so *knew* this was going to happen. I was all like, he wouldn't be so stupid to cheat with me here. Like, no one is that stupid, but I guess you are." She shrugged at Reef then wiggled her fingers me. "You can move again."

Thank you, Lavender. I glared at Reef. *I didn't think my opinion of you could get any lower.*

I don't give a shit what your opinion or anyone else's is. Reef tried to appear tough by expanding his muscles and glaring me. *You have no idea what it means to be an Alpha.*

I wanted to show him but had my own moment of worry when I realized I hadn't practiced, hell, I never used my Alpha power.

How the Fuck am I supposed to do this, I thought.

Jeff answered, *You've always done it by resisting. Put your feelings behind your anger to show that bastard who the real Alpha is.*

Where did you come from?

We've connected, Babe, I'm always here unless you block me. Believe in yourself, and there's nothing you can't—watch out!

Reef rammed me, spinning me away at an awkward angle. My tail went through the specter of Lavender—which mended quickly—and she observed without saying a word. When I stopped turning, I faced Reef and opened myself up to the emotions from as far as I could. The feelings became palpable within my blood with a rush of power and adrenaline. *Your oxygen has to be running out soon, Reef.*

I'm fine. Uncertainty came over Reef's emotions, he didn't know how, but he sensed I was different.

I let all the emotions he had, and everyone else's surge. *Will you still be fine when you stop using your right front flipper?*

Reef's right front flipper laid limp, and his other three needed to work out of sync. *What did you—*

And how about— I thought about the time he forced Maya to irreversibly damage the tip of her own tail because she wounded him. He claimed she tried to murder him—*If Maya was innocent, give yourself her punishment.*

Reef freaked the fuck out, uselessly trying to fight the order of an Alpha. Shaking, with labored breath and grinding his teeth. His efforts fruitless as he moved his tail into position, rocking harder and harder, then he slammed the tip into the ground. Blood shot from all sides clouding the area, scenting the water. He lifted his tail, a third of it barely recognizable. If he didn't weigh five tons the loss of blood would have killed him, but the injury was more like a really bad papercut.

Is this how you want to win, Edi? With cheap parlor tricks? Do you think anyone will respect you when you're Alpha? True predators understand an Alpha is the strongest, bravest, and most ruthless amongst them.

No wonder you suck as an Alpha, you don't know the job description. An Alpha watches over and takes care of all aspects of the shifters lives they rule and helps them progress into the future. We're stuck back fifty fucking years ago.

You have some modern conveniences. You know about the outside world.

Just enough so we don't stick out when in public and draw unnecessary attention to ourselves! Is that not what you said, Reef?

You were safe, that was my job.

Safe from the outside world, but never from you. Your death will be kind considering what you've put us through.

"You don't have to be kind."

What?

"He doesn't have to die, the rules state two go in, one comes out," Lavender said. "I talked to Lucy, you can wish him never to leave the bottom of this lake. He'd spend thousands of years down here by himself. He deserves a fate worse than death, don't you think?"

He'd run out of oxygen.

"Nope, he used his last wish when you shifted as fast as a Lupinski, to breathe underwater."

Planning on keeping me on the bottom until I drown? You're a coward, but I'm not. I wish you the way you were before you dove in, Reef. A flash came from above. I braced myself because Jenn was still Jenn, but nothing terrible happened.

He looked at his fixed tail and moved his unparalyzed flipper. But when he tried to breathe he realized what I really wished for, he couldn't breathe underwater anymore.

My lungs burned, and my thoughts were getting cloudy. I didn't have much time before having to surface so I charged him.

Reacting swiftly, Reef swam towards me. At the last second, he dove to take the cheap shot at my belly. I expected the move, and flipped changing directions and bit into his neck as he passed below. His vertebrae crushed between my jaws, splintering and severing his artery. His blood invaded my mouth, but I squeezed tighter as he jerked twice and then went limp.

I opened my jaws and let him float to the bottom. It took him another moment to turn into a human, then I turned and swam as fast as possible to the surface. I passed Lavender on the way. She nodded then dissipated into little bubbles spreading out like the waves in a puddle becoming more opaque until there wasn't a trace of her. I gnashed my teeth together to stop from inhaling involuntarily and aimed toward the light. Hoping it's the surface and not the light at the end of the tunnel.

Chapter Ten

When my massive head broke the surface, I gasped for air. It probably looked funny: a giant dinosaur flaying about in the water coughing and wheezing. After I caught my breath, I used my back flippers to raise myself out of the water and placed my front fins on the edge of the dock. I shifted back into human, then put my head back into the water to get my hair off my face, and climbed out of the lake and on the dock.

Jeff waited for me with a towel but didn't hand it over until his eyes swept the length of my body. The lust was overwhelming, but he loved me with every ounce of his being as well. He wrapped the towel around me from behind and pulled me close. I kissed him softly; then opened my eyes and backed off an inch when he slammed his mouth on mine and gave me a kiss that made my toes tingle.

No one spoke; they let us have our moment. After we eventually pulled apart, Walt said, "Congratulations, Alpha."

Dread overcame me. I did what was necessary and succeeded in freeing my pod from a tyrant, yet I would be punished for my efforts.

Walt's expression told me I should never be allowed to play poker. "Did you know my brother Nate is older than me?"

"Yes."

"But..." I think he waited for me to say something, but when I didn't, he continued, "...he's not the Alpha."

"No, you are—" *By golly I got it!* "Nate was supposed to be, but you are and—" *Maybe I don't get it.* "I don't know any other details. How did you become Alpha?"

"I willingly gave it up," Nate said as he and his mate Sydney joined us. Andy, the rest of the Lupinskis, Jenn and her family, Lavender, and George joined us too.

"But how? Was it because you're brothers? I'm an only child."

"It doesn't have to be a blood relative—" Walt began.

"Are you saying you could give the control of the entire Lupinski clan to a non-Lupinski?"

"No, of course not, but your situation is different; the guidelines are a bit looser. With the clan's hierarchy, it's inevitable at some point, someone will be born into an ill-suited position, or they don't have the heart and passion for doing it justice. So, abdicating doesn't have too many requirements."

"What are they?"

"It's more of a suggestion, who you choose *should* be a descendant of an Alpha. Shifters chosen—or that win Alpha by combat—without natural abilities or any alpha blood, the results can be disastrous, like with Reef. If there isn't anyone who you deem worthy, you should not abdicate. You need to think long and—"

"I want to abdicate to Seamus." He stood a little straighter. "He would have inherited Alpha after Angus if not for Reef."

"I didn't know Angus had children," Graham said looking at Seamus.

"I'm his great-nephew." Seamus stepped closer to me. "Edi, there's no way of knowing that I would have been chosen for Alpha. There were several candidates—"

"Everyone in the pod knows that it would have been you Seamus. You have all the qualities of an amazing Alpha—"

Seamus interrupted me by putting his hand on my shoulder. "So do you, you'll make a fierce and brilliant Alpha who always puts her home first."

"That's it though, the pod hasn't been my home since dad died. My mom, you guys, Sven, Maria and their kids were all that kept me there." I got a little choked up thinking about the shifters that helped me, and Reef murdered for their efforts. "Only you three are left. I don't hate or blame anyone for what happened or how I was treated, but that doesn't mean I should be the one to try to fix it."

"No one hates or blames you—"

"I know, but they *love* you Seamus. They've treated *you* like their secret Alpha for years, it has to be you. I know that in my soul as much as I know that becoming the pod's Alpha is not the path the Fates designed for me." Jeff put his arm around me. "This is where I belong, it's the home I dreamt of."

"Perhaps, we can make the pod a second home to you once I'm Alpha." I sobbed once Seamus opened his arms, and I walked into them. Lucy and Jenn soon joined us, and we squeezed like it would be the last time we saw each other. All of us wiping away tears when we stepped back.

"So, what do I need to do next?" I asked.

"We wait," said Nate.

"Why?"

"Because the full moon is at its height," Andy said.

Nate spoke, "The actual process of abdicating hurts, it will take you a couple days to recover."

"And you don't need the full moon to gift Seamus your power, but you do need it for a mating ceremony." Ja'Lyn nudged her brother.

Seamus interjected, "I don't mind being interim Alpha for a while. We can make it official whenever you're ready. Have a happy life, it's all we've ever wanted for you."

"Thanks, Seamus, love you."

"Love you too."

I stepped away, and Jeff took my hand, "Are you ready?"

A cool breeze made me realize I was almost naked. "Is there enough time to change? Call me crazy, but I never imagined I'd be rocking a towel at my wedding."

"I can help," Lavender said and wiggled her fingers in our direction.

My towel was replaced with a strapless white-sheer satin sundress with a beaded belt that hugged my hips and trailed behind me. I felt beautiful yet comfortable, perhaps because I was still barefoot.

Jeff looked dashing with cream colored linen pants and a white button-down silk shirt that brought the blue out in his eyes. Lavender didn't stop with us, everyone at the end of the dock wore a new outfit. All the men dressed similarly to Jeff with white linen pants and a variety of colors of silk button down shirts. All the women were in dresses similar to mine but in colors matching their mates. Except for Jenn and George who matched in deep purple but were not mates.

Lavender smiled and said, "You are so beautiful—"

"More than beautiful," Jeff interrupted and I blushed.

"True, but something's missing." Lavender squinted like she was deep in thought, "You need flowers." She snapped and before the sound finished she held a crown made of delicate white flowers and dangling gemstones; the largest stone in the center and at the back was a three-foot piece and sheer white silk for my veil. She motioned for me to bend and put it on my head.

When I stood straight, the shifters around us ooh'ed and ah'ed.

Lavender waited until everyone hushed, "We need more of… like everything." She wiggled her fingers and 'poof' every woman held a bouquet of white and yellow daisies-my favorites. On every dock post, a similar flower arrangement to our bouquets and garlands of white-silk streamed from one to the next all the way to the shore. On dry land, a dance floor, complete with a deejay and a light show. Several smaller portable fire pits with chairs around them, fifty circular ten-person tables with place settings and candelabras surrounded by flowers, and the longest table I had ever seen was covered with food that I could smell from where I stood.

"You should start a party planning business," I said.

"Thank you, but to be honest, I saw it in a magazine last week at the dentist. Everything's ready if you are."

"I am, are you?" Jeff asked.

I nodded my eyes filling with tears, I dreamt of this moment for my entire life, though, I never thought it would happen.

Unlike traditional human weddings, in mating ceremonies, the couples stayed together holding hands forming a circle around us with Walt and Andy in front.

"Are you ready?" Walt asked.

We nodded smiling at one another. Andy stepped closer and held her hands in front of her, palms up. Jeff put his left hand on her right hand, and me my right hand on her left, both palms up.

"Under the light of the full moon, we are here to join two shifters." She moved the hand holding mine like she was closing a book and laid it on Jeff's palm down.

Lavender's eyes went wide and she snapped her fingers, and the beautiful thick braided ribbon I stashed in my bag, one of my most worldly possessions, appeared in Andy's hand.

Shifters understand our mate is chosen by the Fates for a higher purpose. The union is designed to bridge the gap between families and connects you with all the mated pairs before you. This braided ribbon held a single length of material from the bride's dress of every mating it had been used at. More than one-hundred were in mine, the one from my mother's dress on top. This ceremony not only connected Jeff and me to each other, but to all those who came before us.

Andy lay the cord on top of our hands taking one of the ends and wrapping it around our wrists and then did the same with the other. "May your ancestors guide you as you become part of the whole." She squeezed our hands before stepping back.

Walt covered our hands with his own, "May your Clan be there for you as you become one."

Jenn covered our hand with hers. "And may all future generations draw strength from this moment's union. And I wish—"

Oh, shit.

"—you a long, loving, and healthy life together." She was nervous; something would go wrong with her wish, but her tattoos shimmered for a moment, and nothing fell from the sky. We let out sighs of relief and a giggle before she stepped back.

"May the Gods and Goddesses bless you and—" A bright ray of moonlight made our hands glow brightly. There was no denying it, we were true fated mates. The Gods and Goddesses bestowed blessings when their wills followed and this was what it looked like. "—and bind you for all time."

Jeff used his free hand to wrap around my waist and lifted me up to kiss him. I opened myself up to him, and him I. We were one, well almost.

The joy from the crowd was intense, and we broke apart laughing. He put his forehead to mine and whispered, "I love you, Edi."

"I love you, too." He kissed me again and set me on my feet, turned toward the crowd and rose our joined hands together. The hooting and hollering exploded, a mating by the Fates hadn't been seen much until recently, and everyone knew how special it was.

Jeff and I led the way and were inundated with hugs, handshakes, and back slaps. Obligated to make the rounds, but all I could think of was finishing the second half of the ceremony with Jeff, alone, in our home. I could not wait to explore his muscles with my tongue. *Holy shit!* There's still a lot more shifters to say hi to, and I couldn't be thinking this way, or I would drive myself crazy.

"I don't think anyone would mind if you wanted to take off," Walt said. "None of us stuck around mingling when we got hitched. You should go, there's plenty of time to meet everybody, Edi."

"Thank you for everything, Walt." Most of the wedding party gathered closer. "You and Graham saved my ass, by making the contract and bringing Lavender here to bind it."

"Nah that was just insurance—"

"—Tru dat," Lavender interrupted.

"Your win tonight was all you." Walt pulled me in for a hug. "Welcome to the family."

"You can't leave until you hug me too," Jenn said from behind me.

"I would never." I let go of Walt and hugged my best friend.

"I am so happy for you." Jenn squeezed a little tighter before letting go.

"So, if we can leave, how do we sneak out?"

"I can give you a lift. I need to head home—" Lavender checked her watch. "—Poop. I missed curfew. I'm so dead."

"I'll talk to your mom, kid. The timing couldn't be helped, and we owe your coven a debt," Walt assured her.

"That should help, thanks."

"Anytime."

Lavender took our hands, said, "Bye-e!" and the next moment, Jeff and I were outside his house alone.

Chapter Eleven

"Wow, Lavender is better than Lyft," I said. Jeff smiled, she wasn't on his mind, because he opened the door without looking. Then he kissed me softly as he picked me up to carry me over the threshold. His lips never left mine while he carried me through the house and into the bedroom and set me on my feet.

I put my hands on his stomach and felt the strong ridges underneath my fingertips as I slid them up. Needing to lift up to my toes to reach the top button, I kissed under each as I undid them and let the shirt fall to the floor. *Damn.*

Taking my time with kisses, caresses, licks, and small bites on his chest and stomach as my hands explored his softball sized biceps and sinewy forearms. Somewhere in the middle of this, Jeff undid my belt and tossed it aside. He distracted me when he slid his hands down and gently lifted off my dress. He gasped, and I did too when I saw why.

My underclothes were sexy and risqué, like nothing I ever wore before. The white silk and lace strapless bra pushed my boobs up as if gravity didn't exist. Jeff explored my bulging breasts with his eyes, and when he glanced over my shoulder, they were filled with lust. Looking at the mirror behind me, my entire backside on display in a crystal studded G-string. The front didn't leave much to the imagination either, but the garter was what held his attention. He ran a finger across and then snapped it.

"Oh..." The sting surprised me, I liked it. Grinning at my reaction, he lightly kissed my lips before nipping where my neck and collarbone met eliciting another, "Oh!"

Jeff slid his hands down to my hips, pulled me closer, and led me backward until my butt hit the wall. After a smile, he kissed down my body and got on his knees. Eyes level with my breasts, he kissed the skin above each before biting my nipple through the material making me squirm. He did the same to the other before he undid my bra on the first try, then leaned back to watch as he took it off.

Being utterly exposed in more ways than one coupled with the fact I was a virgin, I had a bit of nervousness in the pit of my stomach.

"You're perfect." Jeff kissed above my belly button. "Stop thinking and enjoy, I've been planning tonight since puberty—"

"When was that, like five minutes ago?"

Without a hint, he smacked the side of my ass hard enough to make me jump then rubbed the area in a circular motion, and my eyes rolled.

"You like that?" He slapped the same spot, but leaned in and kissed the area after.

The shakes prevented me from speaking for a second. "I think so, this is—"

"I know, mine too."

"You know? How? And mine too what?"

"I'm a virgin too."

"No way," I looked him up and down.

Jeff shrugged. "Sleeping around never appealed to me, when I knew you'd find me one day."

"Even if it took fifty years? Or never?"

"I have more faith in fate than that." He kissed just under my belly button and touched the top of my panties with the tip of his nose before looking up.

"You ah, don't seem to be stumbling for not having any experience."

"Porn and a recent unhealthy obsession with romance novels."

I laughed.

"I read one of Andy's on a whim, but it turned into a gateway drug to a brand new world for me." Jeff kissed my mound, and I shivered. "Let me show you what I've learned."

Unable to speak, I nodded. Jeff kissed up my belly until he was eye height with my breasts. My nipples hardened under his stare and my breath shortened. Simultaneously he licked one nipple and pinched the other, immediately blowing and lightly touching in kind after. He repeated the process once, then suckled my nipple and continued teasing the other.

When Jeff slid his right hand over my pubic bone to between my thighs, my head fell back and eyes closed.

That's it, let go and enjoy. Jeff's touch was feather-light as he stroked over the entire area. The suckling of one breast stopped as he removed his hand from in between my legs to flick my wet nipple causing me to moan. Then skimmed my stomach with his fingertips before he tugged my panties down and helped me step out of them, trailed back up and began his slow stroking again.

Jeff switched the nipple he was sucking and moved the hand from between my legs to my lips and outlined them, making them wet from my own juices. He used two fingers to pull my bottom lip down and stuck them in my mouth. The other hand pushed a finger inside me.

Moving both hands and sucking at the same time had me shaking within moments. After removing his fingers from my mouth, his hand roamed back to my breast; rubbing, pinching, circling, and squeezing. When my moans became erratic, stopped stroking, kissed my pubic bone, and lifted one of my legs over his shoulder.

Jeff's breath teased my pussy for several long seconds before he licked my clit, sucked hard, and I went weak. Grasping his head to keep from falling, I inadvertently pulled his face in tighter between my legs. He growled in appreciation, and I tightened my grip making him suck and lick harder.

My leg shook, and he responded by putting both his hands under my ass lifting me high enough to hook my other leg over his other shoulder and then he stood. When I was steady against the wall, his mouth went nuts on my core. He licked, nipped, and tugged until I begged for something, I don't know what, I just kept saying 'please.'

One finger, then two stroked something deep inside, and I found out what I needed. Flashes of stars behind my closed eyes while my fingers and toes went numb, and my body shook with relief. Jeff continued his ministrations until my entire body went limp, then he carefully lowered me until my legs slipped down around his waist.

I kissed him ferociously, tasting myself and feeling a new throb in my clit. Hooking my ankles together behind his back, I pulled him in tighter and ground against him. I had no idea what I was doing; it offered some relief, but I needed more. Letting my legs loosen, he could tell I wanted down and stepped back to give me room. As soon as my feet hit the floor, I slid my hands down his arms and over his stomach.

It took two tries to undo his button and lower his zipper. After some tugging and pulling, I managed to push his pants off and to his ankles. Checking out his perfect ass in the mirror, I didn't resist the urge to smack it. He jerked, and his eyes rolled as he groaned.

I put my hands on his hips and turned us until his back was against the wall like mine had been. Kissing, licking, and nipping all over his chest, until he was appropriately squirming. Bypassing his thick cock, I continued kissing down and helped him step out of his pants before licking my way back up.

My right hand cradled his balls as I licked the drop of pre-cum on the tip of his dick making him moan. My left hand grasped the base of his penis. I drew his head into my mouth suckling once or twice before moving back and off again. Opening my mouth wider I sucked the head, and another inch as well into my mouth, a couple short strokes later removed it again. Then I went back and suckled his head for a moment before sliding more of his penis into my mouth.

There was no way for me to fit it all in because he was so long, so I began stroking what I couldn't reach. Moving back, I let the head go, lifted his penis and licked the length of the vein that ran underneath before I took one ball into my mouth.

The noises he made egged me on, I grew wetter and opened my mouth enough to fit both between my lips. His is knees began to shake, and I kept suckling for a couple more moments before letting go and then swallowed his penis as far down my throat as possible. Up and down and up and down I slurped along his shaft while squeezing his balls between my fingers and stroking the base of his dick. As he grew harder in my mouth, I knew he was close, so it surprised me when he moved his hands underneath my armpits and grumbled, "I need to be inside you, now."

Jeff picked me up to meet his mouth for another one of those kisses that could stop time itself. Holding me tight he walked us to the edge of the mattress before he lifted a knee on the bed, and then I helped slide us to the center.

After putting himself in between my legs, he raised my hands near my head and squeezed with enough pressure for me to know he wanted me to stay still. He let my hands go and kissed my breasts, then my belly, sliding his lips all the way down my torso before sitting up. One of his hands moved my knee to the side, so he could stare at my pussy. The hand that pushed my legs open began playing with my clit as his other hand outlined the garter before he snapped it.

I groaned, the sting was incredible. He kissed all the way down to my toes as he slid the garter off. His eyes met mine, and the promise in them excited me more. "I want to do something with you, do you trust me?"

"Of course."

Smiling at my response he lifted himself over me with the garter in his hand. He wrapped it around one of my wrists and twisted, then slid it onto the other, and hooked me to his ornate bed post.

"If you're uncomfortable at all, tell me to stop and I will." I nodded, and he kissed me again before shifting his body and sliding down mine until his head was between my legs.

After kissing both my inner thighs he blew on my ultra-sensitive pussy. His hands slid under my ass and lifted me, and he licked my clit before covering it with his mouth then continued playing with it with his tongue while sucking at the same time.

Squirming and moaning within seconds, I almost cried when he removed his mouth because my orgasm was building. But then he licked my hole as his hand moved around my leg pulling my pussy closer to his mouth. His thumb applied pressure to my nub and made circular motions as he thrust his tongue inside of me.

When I was close, he replaced his thumb with his mouth on my nub and slid two fingers in. Sucking hard he added a third finger, not just moving in and out, but twisting his hand and opening his fingers up near the edge too. I didn't feel my orgasm build this time, instead it exploded within me. He lifted himself from between my legs before slamming and his dick deep inside me.

I gasped when I felt a sharp pain, he held still, and asked, "Are you okay?"

The pain lasted for a few more seconds and then I nodded.

Jeff smiled and began to move so fucking slowly it drove me crazy. "Faster," I groaned without even meaning to, and he obliged.

I was in heaven, but something was missing. "I need to hold you."

He nodded and took off my binding, kissing each wrist before letting me move them to his shoulders. I planted the bottom of my feet on the bed so I could meet him thrust for thrust, demonstrating that I wanted it harder. Soon he was pounding with a greater strength inside me. Hitting my clit with his pubic bone every time he thrust forward making the sensations reverberate. His expression changed and pulled out quickly; then he flipped me over, lifted me so my back was to his front, my legs spread over his lap, and he slid me on his penis.

"Holy shit," I exclaimed, he was so much deeper in this position. My body instinctively knew what to do and began to lift and lower myself on his cock. His hands rested on my hips and helped me get a good rhythm. We stayed this way for a couple seconds, then one of his hands slid to my neck, and pulled me closer. Kissing the space of my neck where it met my collarbone, his teeth grazed my skin, and our thrusting became erratic.

Then his incisors punctured my skin, and he came setting off another orgasm for me, stronger than all the previous ones. It was more than that though, as he sucked my blood; our souls became one. Our mate bond wrapped around each other making two parts greater than the whole.

Eventually, my orgasm subsided, body went limp, and I began to slump over. Jeff wrapped his arms around me and lifted me off him, laying us both down, with my head on his chest. We didn't say anything as our breathing went back to normal. He would occasionally squeeze me tighter, and I did the same.

"I love you, Edi."

"Love you too."

I kissed his chest and put my chin on it so I could look at my mate. We would not always have it easy but whatever we faced, we would, together. I hadn't felt like I belonged anywhere since I was six, but now—

Jeff kissed my forehead, "Welcome home, Edi."

I was home.

Author's Note

Dear Reader-

Thank YOU so much for giving Fateful Wish: Lupinski Clan Book Five a chance! I hope you enjoyed reading it as much as I loved writing Edi and Jeff's story! If you have a moment, please leave a review wherever you picked up your copy. It can be hard as an Indie Author, and reviews from you are essential to our success! Even bad reviews teach us something!

If you'd like to keep up with what's going on in the Lupinski World or me (lol) you can download a FREE book (or more) by signing up for my newsletter. You can do that here: https://www.subscribepage.com/FatefulWishSubscribePage

Until next time…

Emmy

Thanks To...

Atrtink Covers for making Edi come alive on the cover! You should check out their website! Rebecca's work is amazing! https://atrtinkcovers.com/

My Beta Readers, Angela, Rachel, Jackie, and Scarlett, for helping me make Edi & Jeff's story so much better and pointing out when there were too many 'talking heads.'

Kaila Ramos my extraordinary Copy Editor for making sure that no 'waht's' made it through.

My PA's, Erin, Tina, and Jackie for helping me keep sane and being awesome team players that are always willing to help or tell me I'm not the worst writer ever when I'm down.

And my family, my life would be nothing without you! Love you bunches Jon, Prescott, & Hadrian!

Thanks again to YOU for making my dreams come true!

Other Works by Emmy Gatrell:

The Lupinski Clan Series
Romantic Comedies with Happy Endings

Fate is a Mated Bitch: Lupinski Clan 1

A different kind of danger arises when a romance author meets a real life Alpha shifter.

Tall, sexy, smug, confident, and covered in mouthwatering tattoos, Walt Lupinski is determined to bring his Clan out of their 'old way is the best way' mentality that leaves them currently in danger. He can't afford any distractions, let alone a fated mate, to get in the way. Especially when it's against the Good of the Clan law to be with her.

When romance author Andy Cryder discovers her fiancé fulfilling one of his secret desires with their real estate agent, she takes off, not expecting to end up stranded on a desolate mountain...or to be rescued by a group of hot men that look more cut out to be on her book covers than in her real life.

For the first time in her life, Andy feels like she belongs. That is, until their Alpha walks in. What unfolds between Andy and Walt could change everything for the better...or destroy two families for good.

Cords of Fate: Lupinski Clan 2

The Cords of Fate pull them together…

Shifter law tears them apart.

Melanie Cryder and her daughter Samantha have lived full but lonely lives since their mates, Graham and Abe Lupinski, left them because an ancient shifter law forbade them from being together. They've tried to keep Samantha's daughter, Andy, away from them to prevent her from suffering the same fate.

Unfortunately, Andy is driving aimlessly to heal her heartbreak and clear her thoughts. She will eventually make it home to them, she always does. This time, however, the Lupinski's are on the road between them, and they have a nasty habit of getting lost and ending up in Walt's Bar parking lot.

They know they have to rescue her, but will they make it in time?

Forgiving Fate: Lupinski Clan 3

Have you ever known two people clearly attracted to each other, but are forbidden to do anything about it?

Nate Lupinski relinquished his right of becoming the next Alpha of his international multi-shifter clan to pursue his dream of opening a production studio. It's become one of the fastest-growing production companies in the south, and he couldn't have done it without Sydney, a human and his fated mate who can never find out about shifters or could suffer a fate worse than death.

After three years of working her dream job as a Production Coordinator, Sydney Gray is ready to move on. Her undeniable attraction to her boss, Nate Lupinski and her body's betrayal anytime he is near was enough to drive her mad, but his constant flaunting of conquests has broken her heart too many times to count, and she just can't do it anymore.

Just as everything is changing for the Lupinski Clan with the abolishment of the Good of the Clan law, Sydney has decided to leave it all behind. She decided to do one more gig for the company; that's Nate's last chance to convince her to stay.

Will it be enough time for Nate to change her mind, or will it be too late?

Full Moon's Fate: Lupinski Clan 4
A Collection of Short Stories and Novellas
Blurb Coming Soon!

Fateful Wish: Lupinski Clan Book 5

Be careful what you wish for…

Shifter Edi Campbell's wish—not to let memories affect her future— spectacularly backfired and left Edi emotionless and numb to the world. That is until Reef, the pod's Alpha issues a terrible mandate.

For years, Reef terrorized her people into submission, but his declaration that she must become his mate for the Good of the Clan puts Edi's life in jeopardy. Reef's prior mates had a habit of dying shortly after the ceremony.

When members of the pod risk everything to help her escape, Edi flees Scotland, seeking help at Lupinski Clan headquarters in America. There, she meets Jeff Lupinski, an omega whose touch brings back lost feelings, causing her to realize the first wish suppressed more than emotions.

But when Reef shows up demanding surrender—in exchange for her loved ones' freedom—Edi must decide: Will she save the pod by sacrificing her fate to their tyrannical ruler or grasp the power within herself and overcome Reef's evil?

The Daearen Realms Series

Can you imagine a world where science is
replaced with magic?

Meanmna: Book One of the Daearen Realms

**The fate of two worlds rest in one girl's hands, and she doesn't
even know it yet.**

When Seventeen-year-old Sarette begins to see, hear, and feel
things no one else does, along with the vague sensation she's being
watched by some unseen entity, she's ready to commit herself to
the mental hospital. But Elwin, a shiny knight in a worn-out Phish
shirt, has other commitments for her in mind…

Shortly after meeting Elwin, a new life and quest is thrust upon
Sarette. Discovering she is a half-fey princess, she must go on a
dangerous journey through Daearen to Meanmna, the Spirit Realm,
to claim her birthright of becoming High Queen. But if she can't
accomplish the task and restore the balance among the realms, not
only will Daearen fall to darkness…but Earth will be destroyed as
well.

When Sarette leaves everyone and everything she's ever loved
behind, will she have the strength to bring balance or will two
worlds be destroyed?

Bienn-Theine: Book Two of the Daearen Realms

Mathew has a lot on his plate. After finding out that his best friend Sarette is actually his cousin, a fairy, and destined to be queen, he also learns that he's a prince and an heir to the Fire Fey throne. Now instead of applying to colleges and sucking down Boston Coolers in Michigan, he must travel through Daearen to Bienn-Theine, the fire realm, to claim his birthright and fight the dark magic threatening to take all that Mathew holds dear— the woman he has come to adore, Sarette and the family he just found, the fey he has come to love, and the land that becomes home. Mathew must become both a man and a prince to defeat the dark fey threatening the balance between good and evil, not only in the Daearen realms, but on earth as well.

Eitlean: Book Three of the Daearen Realms

Dark magic has spread, gaining traction throughout Daearen and threatening to destroy the balance within the realm—as well as that of Earth. But all may not be lost...

When Banee-Belle of the Air Fey discovers an ancient clue, one which could lead her to the most powerful spells ever written within the realm, hope returns to her heart. If she can employ her wits to decipher the clue, she will gain the ability to wield magic of unheard of power against the Light Fey's evil counterparts. But before her quest even begins, Banee learns she must team up with the one fey who broke her heart, leaving her to live an incomplete life—a fey never made whole.

Can Banee push aside her contempt and distrust to complete her most vital mission yet? Will she have the strength to face her own broken heart to prove she is so much more than the pretty princess everyfey assumes her to be—saving her fey in the process?

Find out in the next thrilling adventure to restore balance within the Daearen Realms.